Bantam Books in the Choose Your Own Adventure® series
Ask your bookseller for the books you have missed

DINOSAUR ISLAND

BY EDWARD PACKARD

ILLUSTRATED BY RON WING

BANTAM BOOKS
NEW YORK · TORONTO · LONDON · SYDNEY · AUCKLAND

RL4, age 10 and up

DINOSAUR ISLAND

A Bantam Book/August 1993

CHOOSE YOUR OWN ADVENTURE® is a registered trademark of Bantam Books, a division of Bantam Doubleday Dell Publishing Group, Inc. Registered in U.S. Patent and Trademark Office and elsewhere.

Original conception of Edward Packard
Cover art by George Wilson
Interior illustrations by Ron Wing

ISBN 0-553-56007-7

Published simultaneously in the United States and Canada

Bantam Books are published by Bantam Books, a division of Bantam Doubleday Dell Publishing Group, Inc. Its trademark, consisting of the words "Bantam Books" and the portrayal of a rooster, is Registered in U.S. Patent and Trademark Office and in other countries. Marca Registrada. Bantam Books, 1540 Broadway, New York, New York 10036.

PRINTED IN THE UNITED STATES OF AMERICA

OPM   0 9 8 7 6 5 4

DINOSAUR ISLAND

WARNING!!!

Do not read this book straight through from beginning to end. These pages contain many different adventures you may have after landing on a remote island in the South Pacific.

From time to time as you read along, you will be asked to make a choice. The adventures you have are the results of your choices. You are responsible because you choose. After you make your decision, follow the instructions to find out what happens to you next.

On the island of the dinosaurs, the only rule is survival of the fittest. Your greatest advantage among these colossal creatures is your human brain, and you'd better be prepared to use it. Otherwise *you* may be the one who winds up extinct!

Good luck!

You've been having a lot of fun being an exchange student in Australia for the past year. Now it's almost time to go home, and you and some of the other kids from your school are on your last scuba diving trip to the Great Barrier Reef. Exploring the strange coral world beneath the sea is a little like visiting another planet.

After an exciting day at sea Nancy Wilson, your dive instructor, and some of the other kids are standing at the rail of your boat as it heads back to the mainland. You notice a plume of smoke on the horizon and point it out to the others.

"That's coming from Kirin Island," Nancy says. "From the volcano."

"Have you ever been there?" you ask her.

She shakes her head. "It's supposed to be very beautiful, filled with rare plants and trees. The island never got developed though. It has no harbors—just coral and sand beaches all the way around."

"Who lives there?"

Go on to page 2.

"Practically no one. The last inhabitants were evacuated years ago. That smoke should tell you why. They say it's just a matter of time before that volcano blows—and when it does it could happen fast."

"I wish I could visit the island," you say. "It would be cool to see an active volcano close up."

"No chance," Nancy says. "A scientific foundation called the Lebeau Institute bought it. It's off-limits to everyone else. They're doing experiments with genetics or something."

Go on to the next page.

The plume of smoke is soon out of sight, and you give no further thought to Kirin Island until a week later when you're preparing to return home. You're watching the news on television one evening, when the newscaster says, "Investigators have learned that scientists at the Lebeau Institute on Kirin Island have made a breakthrough in their efforts to clone dinosaur cells. It may take years more research, but if you're patient, someday you may get to see a real dinosaur." The newscaster smiles and shakes his head as if he doesn't really believe what he's just said.

You don't know whether to believe it either. The next day you ask your science teacher, Mrs. Glass, whether dinosaur cells really could be cloned.

"I guess you heard that news story last night," she says. "Well, the answer is yes—in theory. It could be done by extracting the DNA from dinosaur blood."

"But how could you do that?"

"Of course there's no blood left in any dinosaur fossils. The DNA would have to be taken from veins of amber."

"Amber? How does it get there?" you ask.

Go on to the next page.

She grins. "Mosquitoes. A mosquito bites a dinosaur and sips its blood. Then it alights on some sticky sap oozing out of a tree. It can't escape and is soon encased in the sap. The sap hardens and is later compressed by dirt and rocks. The hardened substance is called amber. The DNA from the dinosaur's blood is preserved within it."

"Then what happens?" you ask Mrs. Glass.

"Millions of years pass. The shape of the land changes. The amber is found in rocks that become exposed," she says.

"And somebody can make a real live dinosaur from that?"

"It wouldn't be easy, but it could be done," your teacher says. "There's a good chance that someday, someone will make a dinosaur."

"It sounds awfully farfetched to me."

"Well, I must say I tend to agree with you," she says. "But remember that before we had computers or VCRs they would have seemed farfetched too."

Turn to page 11.

You eat the food the guard has brought, but the coffee tastes bitter and you put it aside. You go to the window again. This time you notice that there's a vine growing up the wall just outside the window. It gives you an idea. If you can get through the window, you may be able to grab hold of the vine, climb down, and escape into the forest. It's a desperate plan. The vine may give way, and even if it doesn't, you'll have plenty to worry about once you're on the ground. And Lebeau hasn't really done anything to hurt you—yet.

*If you decide to stay in the room,
turn to page 58.*

*If you try to escape,
turn to page 32.*

6

The plane continues to lose altitude. For a couple of minutes there's no further word from the cockpit. Then the pilot comes back on the intercom. "Tighten seat belts, assume bracing position, do not inflate life vests," he says.

You look out the window. You're going down!

You're jerked to the side again as the plane hits the top of an ocean swell, bounces twenty feet into the air, then smacks back down.

Your head snaps forward and hits the seat in front of you. A wing dips into the waves, splitting the side of the plane wide open only a row ahead of you. Then the whole front of the plane plunges down. The tail section, with you, Todd, and Kyra still strapped in your seats, lurches back, exposing the sky in front of you. Water pours in like Niagara Falls. The whole front of the plane is already beneath the waves.

You unbuckle your seat belt and dive to get free. A wave breaks over you, and you go under. When you come up, the part of the plane you were in has already sunk. Someone calls to you. It's Todd! You swim toward him. Kyra is with him. They've got hold of a life raft. The three of you haul yourselves onto it.

Amazingly, your waterproof camera is still strapped to your wrist.

Turn to page 78.

Taking your bearings from the sun, you start off in the direction of the beach where you landed.

It's then that you see a small pack of allosauruses moving across the plain. These creatures are powerfully built, sixteen feet high, with long jaws lined with murderous teeth. They're fiercer looking than you ever could have imagined.

They've been hunting the sauropods near the forest's edge and don't appear to notice you, except for one baby allosaurus that has strayed from the pack. It spots you and immediately charges—even though you're still a quarter of a mile away!

You're both terrified and fascinated. The baby allosaurus is no larger than a grizzly bear, but it has a set of teeth more deadly than those of a great white shark.

The animal wobbles as it runs—it can't be more than a few weeks old. Maybe you can scare it away, or at least dodge it.

You glance around and find a stick to use as a club. You brandish the stick in the air and shout. The allosaurus stops, looking confused. You have to laugh.

Then it comes at you again, wobbling even more, looking as if it won't even know what to do when it reaches you.

It knows.

The End

"I agree with Kyra," you say. "It can't be more than a hundred miles to the mainland. We should be able to make it in a day or so if we get a good wind."

"I guess the majority rules," Todd says with a shrug.

You hoist the sail, and the raft begins moving quickly over the waves. You look back at the area around the crash site, but all that's left to see are a thin slick of oil and a few pieces of floating debris marking the spot.

The rest of the day passes uneventfully. There's enough food and water on board to last about a week, and you're sure you'll reach land long before that. When darkness falls, the three of you agree to take turns steering the raft and keeping watch.

Go on to the next page.

10

You're awakened by Todd at dawn the next morning. "Bad news," he says. You sit up and look around. A dense fog has closed in. The wind has dropped, and the sail is flopping back and forth as the raft bobs in the waves.

You peer out into the grayness, then lean over the side and swish your hand through the water. It feels quite warm.

Turn to page 95.

You soon forget all about dinosaurs as you finish up your year in Australia. You've had fun, but you're excited about heading home. You and two friends from America, Kyra Bohlen and Todd Harris, have reserved seats together on the plane.

You're a little worried though. A lot of flights have been canceled lately because of exceptional sunspot activity. Most scientists say that solar storms of this kind are just part of a cycle that happens every once in a while. However, they admit that this may be the worst in hundreds of years. The sunspots have been sending tremendous bursts of cosmic rays into space, causing beautiful aurora displays at night but also making television images turn into waving, fluttery lines and interfering with electronic navigation systems.

Turn to page 50.

12

Fifteen minutes later the boat rounds a point and passes between a pair of breakwaters arranged to form an artificial harbor. Then it slows and glides into a dock between a speedboat and a small cabin cruiser that are already parked there.

The men lead you to a concrete building that looks like a cross between a fortress and a resort hotel. There are no windows on the first floor, but there is a spacious veranda on the floor above. Flowering vines cover much of the surface of the concrete walls. An armed guard stands near the entrance.

"This is like some small island republic run by a dictator," Todd whispers to you.

"Maybe that's what it is," you whisper back.

When you reach the door, a short, sixtyish man with wisps of white hair strides forward to meet you. In his gaudy flower-print shirt, he looks more like a tourist than a dictator.

"I'm Claude Lebeau," he says. He speaks with a heavy French accent.

The three of you introduce yourselves.

"They radioed me from the patrol boat about you. I'm happy you're safe," he says. "Come into my office a moment. Then I'll see that you get a good meal and a shower."

Turn to page 96.

14

Arturo points to a lever on the dashboard of the boat. "It's very simple. Forward, neutral, and reverse. When I cast you off, move it forward." He indicates another lever. "That's the throttle. Right now it's set on idling speed. Keep it barely above that as you're pulling out of the harbor or you'll make too much noise. About a quarter of a mile out, you can increase your speed. But don't go too fast. Hit a wave wrong, and you'll flip the boat. Got it?"

"Got it. But which way do I steer?"

He points to a dimly illuminated dial on the dashboard. "There's your compass. Just head due west. When you reach land, beach the boat. You won't have enough gas to search for a harbor. Now let's go." He jumps back onto the dock, casts off the lines, and motions for you to put the engine in gear.

You move the lever forward. A siren goes off, wailing in your ears.

Turn to page 23.

You start back toward Arturo. You've almost reached him when you feel the ground shuddering. You keep running, but the ground is giving way under your feet.

You slip and slide into a ditch, turning your ankle as you land. A stabbing pain cripples you completely.

You lie there panting for breath. You need to tape your ankle. You need ice.

But suddenly it doesn't matter. The whole top of the mountain explodes. Seconds later, the hot, poisonous blast sweeps over you and everything else. In an instant the island is changed from the realm of creatures living in the past to the realm of creatures not living at all.

The End

16

The beach is bathed in golden light from the sun, which is just about to rise. The view inland is blocked by high bluffs running along the coast.

"I hope this island is inhabited," Kyra says.

"An island this size has got to be," Todd says.

"Maybe not," you say, pointing. "Look at that smoke. I bet this is Kirin Island."

"The one that's too dangerous for people," Todd says.

"That's right," you say. "Except for the scientists of the Lebeau Institute. I'm sure they have a helicopter that can take them out of here in a hurry."

"If the volcano hasn't blown for decades, I don't think it will just because we landed here," Todd says.

"Look!" Kyra exclaims suddenly.

You look where she's pointing. A boat is racing by. Three men are standing in it. Two are armed with machine guns, and the third is holding a bazooka.

If you duck down and keep out of their sight, turn to page 34.

If you try to get their attention, turn to page 91.

18

The two of you slip through the gate behind the brush, hoping the guard won't notice you. But apparently he does, for he comes out of the guardhouse and trains his binoculars in your direction. You and Rosanna duck out of sight, and after a few minutes the guard returns inside. Seconds later a heavy steel bar swings down across the gate. You're trapped!

Rosanna sighs and shakes her head. "Well, we might as well make the best of it."

Turn to page 56.

You have more questions, but Pierre hustles you out of the room and off to the cafeteria so fast you don't have a chance to ask them.

"This place is totally bizarre," Todd says when you're seated.

"Do you think there really are dinosaurs here?" Kyra says.

You shrug. "I don't know, maybe. But I don't think the radio is as dead as Lebeau claims it is."

After you eat, Pierre leads you all down into the basement, then through a tunnel that runs several hundred yards underground. He explains that you are passing beneath the electrified fence that encloses the dinosaurs. A few minutes later you surface in a concrete blockhouse with tiny steel-barred windows. Pierre opens a heavy steel door.

Turn to page 24.

You, Kyra, and Todd follow the pair up the gully to the bluff above it. From the top you have a clear view of a semiwooded plain, with the cone-shaped volcano beyond it. The plume of smoke is still coming out the top. You turn back to the strangers.

"Who are you?" you say. "And who were those men in the patrol boat?"

"I'm Arturo Scarlatti and this is my colleague Rosanna Gallo. I'm a zoologist and Rosanna is a geologist. We landed in a Sabercraft—a fast, little boat you can bring right up on the beach. We hid it in a creek that runs into the ocean about a half mile from here."

The three of you introduce yourselves and tell Arturo and Rosanna about your escape from the plane crash. "But why are you here?" you ask Arturo.

"I said that we're scientists, and that's true," he says. "But we are also spying."

"Spying? How come?"

"The Lebeau Institute is breeding dinosaurs on this island."

"You're kidding," you say, as Kyra and Todd gasp in disbelief.

"Not at all—we've seen a number of them."

You gaze off at the tree-dotted plain.

Turn to page 79.

22

"We spotted a group of twelve sauropods through the fence," Arturo says. "We don't know what else there is. Lebeau has been cloning several species, but we think the others may only be in the embryo stage."

"Are sauropods meat eaters or plant eaters?" Kyra asks.

"Plant eaters," Arturo says. "No use hatching predators until you have something to prey on, right?"

"But don't think you can't get hurt by one of these plant eaters," Rosanna adds. "They're thirty feet high, and they may not like strangers invading their habitat."

"Besides, there may be predators too," Arturo says. "Lebeau may be further along than we think."

"What do we do next?" you wonder aloud.

"I'm pretty sure we can help you take one of Lebeau's speedboats," Rosanna says. "The sea is calm—it should only be about a twenty-hour trip to the mainland."

"What about you two?" Todd asks.

"Don't worry about us," she says. "Arturo and I are determined to see everything that's on this island and get our own film footage. We're willing to risk our lives to do it. You can come with us if you want, and we'll do our best to protect you. But I think you'd be wiser to try to escape by boat."

Turn to page 97.

It's too late for second thoughts. Arturo is already running for the woods. You give the engine the throttle, snake around the dock, and turn toward the end of the breakwater.

Shots ring out. Bullets spatter all around you. You shove the throttle forward to full power and are thrown back in your seat as the boat leaps ahead, bow high out of the water. This boat is like a wild horse—you can't keep on course. That may be just as well, since bullets are hitting all over the place. One hits the dashboard, smashing the radio and the compass.

Turn to page 35.

24

The three of you step outside. The sun is barely showing through the yellowish haze that hangs over the island.

"Enjoy the dinosaurs," Pierre says. He returns inside the blockhouse, shutting the door behind him. You try the handle, but it's locked.

"We're inside the electrified fence," Kyra says.

"That means there's nothing between us and the dinosaurs," Todd says. He looks around.

Suddenly the ground rumbles under your feet.

"An earthquake," Kyra says. Even as she speaks, the rumbling stops, but you don't feel relieved. Looking up at the volcano, you can see tongues of flame in the yellowish smoke above the summit.

Kyra points out over the plain, and you see several dinosaurs with enormously long necks and tails and greenish-dappled skin.

"Sauropods," Kyra says. "But I don't know what kind."

"Neither do I, but I think I've seen their pictures in books," Todd says. "I didn't know they'd be so green."

"No one knew," Kyra says. "Fossils don't preserve color."

"They're plant eaters," you say. "I don't think they'll attack us."

"Maybe, maybe not," Kyra says. "We don't know how they'll behave. Besides, the volcano seems to be acting up. We've got to get out of here."

Turn to page 101.

"I was a black-beret sharpshooter," Arturo says. "I'll hit them. Afterwards we'll get one of the boats. The speedboat would be much faster, but I happen to know that it has a security alarm on it. That could cause trouble. It might be wiser to take the cruiser, but the decision's up to you."

You're thinking about what to do when Kyra whispers, "I want to talk to you alone."

"We're going to talk about it," you tell Arturo.

Kyra leads you off a few paces. "How do we know we can trust Arturo?" she whispers. "He may just be trying to use us. We have no proof that Lebeau will hurt us. Just because he has security guards doesn't mean he's a criminal. But we'll be criminals if we let Arturo tranquilize the guard and we steal the boat. We could end up in jail."

Arturo is walking toward you. "C'mon, kids. It's almost dark now. We can't waste any more time."

Kyra looks first down at the harbor, then at you. Taking a deep breath, she says, "I don't want to steal the speedboat, and I don't want to get any closer to those dinosaurs."

"Well, what *are* you going to do?" Arturo asks.

"I don't think anyone is going to hurt me. I'm just going up to the main building."

"What will you tell them about the rest of us?" you ask her.

Turn to page 47.

"I want to get out of here," you say. "I'll try to escape."

"Me too," Kyra says.

"I guess I'll stay on the island," Todd says. "This could be the only chance I get to see a real live dinosaur."

"All right," Arturo says. "Todd, you wait here with Rosanna. I'll take these two to one of Lebeau's boats and be back in about an hour."

You and Kyra follow Arturo along a path on the crest of a bluff overlooking the sea. You've walked about a mile when Arturo motions for you to stop.

"Wait here," he says.

Go on to the next page.

You watch while he climbs a little ridge and scans the area ahead with binoculars. After a second he looks back and motions for you and Kyra to join him.

The sun has set and the light is fading, but from the top of the ridge you can see a fortresslike building in the distance. Arturo hands you the binoculars and points to a large cage near the main building. In it are two animals about the size of cows—but they certainly aren't cows.

"Baby brachiosauruses," Arturo says. "Just

out of their eggs. It will be a week or so before they're old enough to be released in the wild."

"It's hard to believe, even though I'm looking right at it," you tell Arturo.

Turn to page 54.

Lebeau has a smug smile on his face. "Understand this, my young friend. The dinosaurs are mine. If I don't want anyone else to see them, that is my business."

"I think it's everybody's business," you say. "Something this important should be done for the whole world, not just for the whim of one man."

"That is *your* view," Lebeau says. "But I own this island and my view is the one that is dominant here."

This argument is going nowhere. Besides, something else is on your mind. "May I use a phone?" you say. "I want to call my parents and let them know I'm alive."

"Communications are out right now. You can call them when you get back to the mainland," Lebeau says. "I'll put you on the next helicopter flight out of here, first thing tomorrow. Meanwhile, would you like to see the dinosaurs?"

"Sure, but what about my friends? Are you going to—"

"We'll find them and bring them in. They will be perfectly safe. Now, Andre here will give you some refreshment. Then you can see the animals."

Go on to the next page.

He nods at a guard, who shows you into a small cafeteria farther down the hall. The guard brings you a sandwich and a soda. You haven't even finished them when you begin to feel sleepy. Unable to hold your eyes open, you slump back in your chair.

Turn to page 71.

32

After some effort, you manage to pry the window open. Then you grit your teeth and leap for the vine, almost pulling it off the wall. You slide down before it gives way completely and run toward the fence. But you stop just short of it, remembering that there's enough voltage in it to hold back a dinosaur.

You walk along the fence, hoping to find your friends. You've gone about a mile when you catch sight of an allosaurus inside the fence. It's a sixteen-foot-high monster that would terrify any animal on earth.

The allosaurus sees you and lets out a bellow that rattles your bones. You're on the outside of the fence, but the dinosaur doesn't seem to care. It charges with ten-foot strides, crashes into the fence, and brings it to the ground. Electricity crackles. Sparks cascade fifty feet into the air.

The monster is fatally burned, yet still alive. Consumed by anger, it keeps coming.

You run and dive again to avoid its upraised claws. Then you glance over your shoulder and get your last look at a dinosaur—very close up.

The End

You duck behind a small dune. "Get down!" you tell the others. They obey, and the boat goes by.

Todd looks at you angrily. "Why did you do that? They would have rescued us."

"Or arrested us, or worse," you say. "Didn't you see those weapons?"

Todd shakes his head. "That was dumb. We're on a strange tropical island with no food and no supplies. If we're not willing to take a chance with whoever controls the island, how do you expect to be rescued? I wish I hadn't listened to you."

"Stop arguing," Kyra says. "We've got to decide what to do."

Turn to page 46.

You manage to keep control of the wheel as the boat slaps into a wave, takes off into the air, slams onto another wave, and tilts half on its side. You lean the other way, afraid the boat is going to flip, but it settles on an even keel.

You throttle down a little now that you're out of firing range. Then you take some deep breaths, trying to relax as the island recedes in the distance. Finally you lose sight of it. Darkness is coming on rapidly. Your biggest problem now is that your compass is out. You'll have to navigate by the stars. You look around the sky, searching for the North Star, but you don't see it. Then you remember that it can't be seen this far south.

There's another star you can use for a guide. Even though it's close to the horizon, it's so bright that you're sure it's the planet Venus. It must just have risen or be about to set, and therefore it must be either in the east or the west.

If you head toward Venus, turn to page 110.

If you head away from it, turn to page 45.

"I want to take the speedboat," you tell Arturo. "Kyra, will you come with me?"

"I'll stay here," she says in a low voice.

"All right, wait here, Kyra—I'll be watching you," Arturo says. He loads his rifle with tranquilizer darts. Then, motioning for you to follow him, he starts down the path to the harbor.

You've traveled about half the distance when the dogs get up and start sniffing at something along the edge of the dock. The guard gets to his feet and watches them. When you're about a hundred yards away, Arturo raises his rifle and fires. The only sound is the muffled report of the rifle. The guard drops to the ground. As the dogs start to investigate the fallen guard, Arturo fells them with successive shots.

You shudder. "Are you sure—?"

"I'm sure," Arturo says. "They'll be okay. Come on."

You follow him down the path and out onto the dock. He hops aboard the speedboat. You climb aboard as well and watch as he tinkers with the ignition. A second later the engine comes to life.

Turn to page 14.

38

You dodge sharply, like a football player trying to avoid a tackler. But even a baby tyrannosaurus is used to this tactic—lots of small mammals try it. It brings you to the ground with a nudge of its oversize head.

Your last sight is of a set of tremendous jaws closing around your head.

The End

"Come on, Arturo," you say. "I want to take the cruiser." You look at Kyra. "Are you sure you don't want to come?"

She shakes her head. Arturo tells her to wait for him. He fires his tranquilizer gun at the guard and dogs, and leads you aboard the cabin cruiser. He starts the engine and shows you how to work the controls.

"Good luck, kid." He casts off the lines. You ease the throttle gently forward and steer the boat out of the harbor. When you're clear of the breakwater, you speed up.

It's not until you've been underway for about half an hour that you think to look at the gas gauge. There's only a quarter tank left. You know that won't be enough to reach the mainland. You cut the throttle to save fuel.

Not long afterwards you hear the sound of an engine in the distance. A minute or two later you make out the shape of the boat coming toward you. It's Lebeau's speedboat!

The faster craft pulls alongside the cruiser. Two men wearing military fatigues and armed with automatic rifles climb onto the cruiser.

"Take the boat back to dock," one says.

You turn the wheel. "You don't need to point that gun at me," you say.

"It has to point somewhere," he says.

The other man laughs. You realize you'd better do as they say.

Turn to page 89.

40

You give Kyra a hug and tell her you'll send help as soon as you can. Then you shinny up the tree, rock it until you're over the fence, and let go. You hit the ground hard. Your ankle gives way, and a stabbing pain runs up your leg.

Todd runs over to help. He looks at your ankle, which is already swelling. You try to get up, but the pain is too great to put any weight on your injured leg.

"I wish I could carry you, but you're too heavy," Todd says.

"You go ahead," you say. "Maybe you can find the boat and make it to the mainland."

Todd pats your shoulder. "I'll send help as soon as I can." He waves to you and to Kyra, who's been watching through the fence. Then he turns and takes off at a trot.

"Sorry about what happened to you," Kyra says through the fence.

"I don't know who's worse off," you say. "You stuck on that side with the dinosaurs, or me stuck on this side with a bum leg."

You soon find out. A poisonous adder—only three feet long, but deadly as any dinosaur—is slithering toward you. You see it in time to run. But that's the one thing you can't do.

The End

Soon afterward you see a great hump in the sea coming toward you. The boat rises up a hundred feet in the air, hangs on the crest, then slides down the back of the wave, hitting the trough with a jolt that pitches you sharply forward.

Todd cries out as his elbow bangs against a thwart. You grab the wheel and struggle to steady the helm as Kyra is flung aside.

"How's your elbow?" you ask Todd when you've got the boat under control.

"I'm going to have a bruise, but it'll be okay," he answers.

"Hey," Kyra exclaims. "We made it. We survived the eruption!"

"And the dinosaurs," you say.

"And Claude Lebeau," Todd adds.

You set the boat on course toward the mainland, knowing you're going to make it home. Not only that—you've got a roll of dinosaur pictures in your camera.

The End

Rosanna stands with her arms folded, an anguished look on her face. "We've got to get Arturo to come with us," she says.

"Let's give him a final warning," you suggest.

"I have the keys to the engine of the boat," Rosanna says. "If I warn him, he may take them away from me."

"Then let's just go," Todd says.

Rosanna still looks uncertain.

You feel the ground trembling under your feet. A sound fills the air, so low pitched you can hardly hear it, yet you feel it in your bones.

"I'm getting out of here even if I have to swim for it," Kyra says.

You feel the same way as Kyra, but you don't feel right about leaving Arturo. Should you urge the others to leave now, or to give Arturo one more chance to change his mind? Time is running out.

If you urge the others to leave immediately, turn to page 66.

If you run after Arturo, turn to page 76.

You head toward a star in the opposite direction from Venus. The sea is calm, and the boat cuts smoothly through the water.

After a while you see a glow on the horizon ahead of you. Could it be land? You speed up, eager to reach your goal. Gradually, the lights and outline of the land come into view. It's Kirin Island! You've been going the wrong way! You instantly spin the wheel, hoping that no one on-shore has spotted you.

You've gone about a mile when you hear a sound above you, louder than your own engine. You look up and see the silhouette of a helicopter. A moment later you're blinded by floodlights. You swerve the boat, but not in time to avoid the bullets raining down from the sky.

The End

46

For the rest of the day you stay close to the beach, hoping a more friendly boat will pass by. You find a freshwater spring and nibble on some strange-looking fruit from a nearby tree. Late in the day, a whistle sounds from the bluff overhanging the beach. You look up and see two people, a rugged-looking young man with several days' growth of beard and an athletic-looking woman about the same age. They're both wearing khaki shorts and carrying lightweight backpacks. Your first impulse is to run, but then you see that they are armed only with binoculars and cameras.

They walk along the top of the bluff and then climb down a gully where the slope is not so steep. You step forward to meet them. "Where did you kids come from?" the man asks.

"Our plane crashed," Todd says. "I think we were the only survivors."

"How awful," the woman says. "But come with us—hurry. They're patrolling this island by boat. If they spot you, you're dead."

Turn to page 21.

"She isn't going to tell anyone anything about the rest of us," Arturo says. He lays a hand on her shoulder. "Kyra, I can't let you do that. If you don't want to risk taking a boat, you'll have to come back with Rosanna and me and your friend Todd."

"You just don't want them to know you're spying!" Kyra says.

"Yes, that's part of it," Arturo says, "But I also want to do what I can to protect you kids."

"I don't want to be stuck here alone. Please stay with me," Kyra whispers to you.

By this point you're feeling very confused. You're not sure what to do. But Kyra and Arturo are both watching you, waiting for your decision.

If you decide to try to take the speedboat, turn to page 36.

If you decide to try to take the cruiser, turn to page 39.

If you decide to go to the headquarters building, turn to page 73.

If you decide to stay with Arturo and Rosanna, turn to page 59.

48

"What made you think you had a right to steal my boat?" Lebeau asks when you finish.

"I was scared," you say. "Arturo said you'd kill us if you caught us. I just wanted to get away."

"I would kill you?" Lebeau shakes his head. "What an absurd accusation. Why should you trust someone who says such a thing?"

"Because Arturo and Rosanna are scientists."

"How do you know?"

"Because they had cameras and camcorders instead of guns."

"That's a joke," Lebeau says. "What about that rifle?"

"It only shoots tranquilizer darts," you say.

"Oh, really? Then why are one of my guards and two of my dogs dead?"

You are shocked to hear this. Could it be that Arturo lied to you? That he shot the guard and the dogs with real bullets?

"It disgusts me," Lebeau continues. He picks up the phone and says something into it in French. Then he gets up and walks halfway around his desk. "Jacques," he says to one of the guards, "put this kid in room twelve."

"I need to use a phone," you say.

Go on to the next page.

"In good time," Lebeau replies. He motions to the guards. One of them takes you upstairs and shows you into a small bedroom.

"We're going to lock you in for the night. Knock on the door if you want to go to the bathroom," the guard says.

"Wait—"

Turn to page 100.

50

Right up until the last minute you're not sure whether your flight will take off or not. You, Kyra, and Todd, sitting in the last row in the plane, give a little cheer as the wheels leave the ground.

The plane has only been in flight for a few minutes, however, when an announcement comes from the pilot. "There's reported turbulence ahead," he says. "We want to give you folks a nice smooth ride, so we're altering course to avoid it. As a precaution, though, please keep your seat belts securely fastened."

Seconds later the plane hits an air pocket and drops like a rock. Your small waterproof camera almost flies out of your hand. You decide to strap it to your wrist.

"Sorry about that, folks," the pilot says over the intercom. "Things should be smoother ahead, but unfortunately we're experiencing an electrical problem. Navigation's out, and so is the radio, so we're returning to the airport. No need to worry—we have plenty of fuel."

For a moment you feel relieved. Then the plane hits another wild patch of air. You're wrenched savagely to one side, and your seat belt digs into your stomach. The plane sinks, then rises dizzily, then sinks again.

People gasp. Someone lets out a scream.

Turn to page 6.

52

"I've been wondering that too. It's awfully weird that there's been no mention of anything except your research with cells on TV or in the newspapers," Kyra says. "I would think lots of reporters would be visiting you, wanting to know what's going on."

"That's exactly why it's so secret," Lebeau replies. "I have been conducting a great experiment—recreating the world as it was a hundred million years ago. That experiment would be ruined if planes were flying overhead and reporters and curiosity seekers landing on the beaches."

"When are you going to let people know about this?" you ask.

"As soon as I've gathered the necessary data." Lebeau rises from his chair. He motions to a man standing in the doorway. "Now, Pierre will take you for some breakfast in the cafeteria. Then he'll show you to the dinosaur observation post. You're in for quite a surprise, I can assure you."

Turn to page 19.

With all of you bailing, you're able to get most of the water out of the boat in a couple of minutes.

"Well, we survived," Todd says.

"We did." Rosanna's voice breaks. "But not Arturo. We should have tried harder to get him to come."

"I'm sorry," you say.

"I'm sorry too," says Kyra. "But ten more minutes and we might not have made it."

"It was Arturo's decision," Todd says. "We shouldn't feel guilty."

"You're right," Rosanna says. "We should mourn him, but not feel guilty."

No one says anything for a while. Then Rosanna lets out a cry. "I just noticed. The wave carried off all our supplies, all my film, cameras, notes—everything!"

"That's awful," you say.

Turn to page 68.

54

"I feel the same way," Arturo replies. "But we've got other things to think about right now." He points to some coral jetties that have been built out on the water to form an artificial harbor. Two boats are tied up at a dock within this harbor. One is an open speedboat, the other a small cabin cruiser. A man in camouflage gear is sitting on a bench near the dock. A pair of guard dogs—Dobermans—are stretched out nearby.

"They have two other boats," Arturo says. "A big one that was sent to the mainland this morning for supplies, and the patrol boat you saw just after you landed on the island. The patrol boat circles the island four times a day. It won't be back to the dock for a couple of hours."

"How can we get past the guard and the dogs?" you ask.

Arturo pulls a rifle from his pack.

"You're going to shoot them?" Kyra exclaims with a gasp.

Arturo shakes his head. "I don't believe in killing people or animals. This rifle is loaded with tranquilizer darts. The guard and those dogs will be asleep before they know what hit them."

Go on to the next page.

Kyra looks worried. "How do you know what dose to give?"

"Long experience with animals in the wild," Arturo says. "The guard gets the same dose as a male chimp—they're about the same weight. The dogs get two-thirds as much."

"Can you be sure you'll hit them?" you ask.

Turn to page 26.

The two of you set out through the pine grove, just inside the fence following the slope to the top of the hill. The weather is oppressive. A yellowish haze hangs over the island and the sulfurous taste of the air sticks in your throat. You want to see the dinosaurs—but more than that, you want to get off this island.

After a hard climb, your feet aching, your clothes drenched with sweat, and your canteens almost empty, you and Rosanna reach the top of the hill. Ahead of you is a lake surrounded with long fernlike grass. Two sauropods are standing knee-deep in the water, drinking.

About half a mile to the right of the pond several hadrosauruses, each about thirty feet long, are browsing at a clump of trees.

A shadow moves across the meadow. You look up and see a pterosaur, a flying reptile with a thirty-foot wingspan.

Turn to page 87.

58

You decide to stay in the room and take your chances with Lebeau. At least you're fed and cared for here—in fact your bed is quite comfortable. And you're sure that the next time Lebeau sends a boat or helicopter to the mainland you'll be on it.

A few minutes later, you're startled by a low rumbling sound. You spring up and look out the window again. The smoke from the volcano is even thicker. An acrid smell hangs in the air.

About midmorning you hear muffled explosions coming from the volcano. Through the gaps in the trees you see a large helicopter rising from the plain. Within seconds the top of the volcano bursts open. The whole mountain blazes with fiery light.

The helicopter swerves violently, then breaks apart in midair. Seconds later superheated air, traveling close to the speed of sound, flattens the entire island, destroying everything on it—including you.

The End

"I guess it's too risky to try to escape. I'll stay here with you guys," you say.

"All right, follow me, and keep up. We've wasted too much time already." Arturo breaks into a trot, and it's all you and Kyra can do to keep up with him.

When you reach the top of the ridge, you spot Rosanna and Todd waiting where you left them. Arturo starts to call to them, but Rosanna, seeing you, puts a finger to her lips. She points across the meadow. In the fading light, you see a baby sauropod, about the size of an Indian elephant, standing there. It's the cutest animal you've ever seen, if anything so big could be called cute. You wonder where its mother is.

Rosanna trains her video camera on the dinosaur while you start taking pictures of it with your waterproof camera. A few moments later the baby dinosaur catches sight of you and starts lumbering toward you. You quickly realize that if the animal keeps coming, it will run right into the electric fence. Arturo races toward the dinosaur, shouting. It stops and looks at him, startled, and you get two or three more good pictures. Then it backs away.

Like a moving mountain, the baby's mother appears from behind a stand of trees. You've seen a skeleton of a sauropod in a museum, so you had some idea how big they were, but nothing has prepared you for the sight of the living creature.

Turn to page 92.

Arturo moves closer to Rosanna. "What do you think?" he asks.

She pulls the rod out of the ground and begins packing up the instrument. "I think we'd better get off this island."

"Not until we get all these dinosaurs on film," he says, turning away.

"Is that more important to you than our lives, and those of these children?" Rosanna's face is flushed with anger.

He raises his voice. "We agreed, remember? We'll take our chances and stick it out."

"That was before I thought this mountain was going to blow up."

The two of them argue for a few more minutes, then Arturo says, "We'll just walk the length of the fence, then quit."

"That's eight miles," Rosanna exclaims.

He answers by strapping on his pack and starting off along the fence.

A low rumbling sound fills the air. Arturo stops and looks up at the volcano. Yellowish smoke, laced with tongues of flame, is rising from the summit. Steam is seeping from widening cracks along the base of the mountain.

"Does that convince you?" Rosanna yells after him.

Go on to the next page.

He looks back over his shoulder. "We have a job to do, Rosanna."

She turns to you and your friends. "He's lost all perspective. It's suicidal to stay on this island."

"Then let's take the Sabercraft and get out of here," Todd says.

Turn to page 75.

62

You drop your pack and race toward Lebeau's headquarters. If you make it, you won't need any supplies. If you don't, it won't matter.

On and on you run, but it's much farther than you'd thought. You have to stop several times to catch your breath.

You hear a loud sound ahead. Mustering up a last burst of speed, you break into the clearing just in time to see a helicopter taking off. It rises straight up a hundred feet, then veers east.

Seconds later the sky lights up. The volcano has turned into a mountain of fire. Through the thickening smoke you see the helicopter swerve, roll, burst into flame, and then explode into a thousand pieces. You've barely had time to take in this spectacle when the blast of superheated air, traveling almost at the speed of sound, reaches you.

The End

"I can't get back inside," Todd calls across the fence. "Maybe I could steal a tractor or something and knock down the fence."

"You'd just get caught," Kyra says. "You should take the boat and try to get help."

"I guess you're right," Todd says. His eyes meet yours. "What about you? Are you coming with me or staying with Kyra?"

You hate the thought of leaving Kyra alone. "I guess I'd better stay here," you say.

"I sure could use your help with the boat," Todd says. "I don't know if I can make it to the mainland all by myself."

*If you decide to go with Todd,
turn to page 40.*

*If you decide to stay with Kyra,
turn to page 111.*

One of the men helps you and Kyra aboard. Then the helmsman whirls the boat around and heads out to sea.

"Can't we go back to the island?" you ask. "We want to find our friend."

The second man points at the smoldering volcano. "We just have to hope your friend found another boat. If we went back now, we'd never get away. That volcano is about to explode. We know—we've been taking measurements."

"What were you doing here?" you ask. "Looking for the dinosaurs?"

"Dinosaurs?" he says with a chuckle. "That's just a rumor about this island. We're volcanologists. We were trying to measure seismic effects as close to the time of the eruption as possible."

"But there *are* dinosaurs on that island. We saw them!"

The helmsman pats your shoulder. "Sure, kid. Sure there are."

The End

66

"We've got to escape right away," you say. "We can't save Arturo by staying here. We'll just sacrifice our own lives along with his."

Rosanna stands with her arms crossed, her eyes on Arturo, who is still up on the ridge. "I just don't feel right about this," she says.

You put your hand on her shoulder. "Rosanna, you said yourself that it would be suicide to stay here. Now let's go while there's still time."

She doesn't answer for a few moments, but then she sighs and picks up her backpack. With a last glance at Arturo, she starts down the slope toward the beach. You, Todd, and Kyra follow her down the narrow trail.

By the time you reach the creek where the Sabercraft is hidden, the smoke from the volcano is even denser. It's getting hard to breathe. The four of you haul the Sabercraft out of the brush, launch it into the creek, and climb aboard. Rosanna starts the engine and heads the boat toward the choppy waters where the creek feeds into the ocean.

Fortunately, the sea is fairly calm, and you're able to put on plenty of speed. Within an hour you're almost twenty miles away. The island is no more than a smoky shape on the horizon.

Suddenly, the sky above it turns into fire.

"It's blown!" Rosanna shouts. "Get down!"

The three of you crouch in the bilge. Rosanna grips the wheel.

Turn to page 115.

Rosanna shakes her head in disbelief. "If only I had even one roll of film. But I have nothing— no record to prove what we saw!"

"We have our memories," Kyra says. "We can give eyewitness accounts of what we saw."

"I have something better than that," you say. You hold up the waterproof camera still strapped to your wrist.

Rosanna's face brightens. "You got some pictures?"

"Almost a whole roll," you say.

It's only then that you all notice the mountain of water moving toward the boat. It's a great wave, set off by the earthquake that accompanied the volcano's eruption. Moments later the raft rises high in the air, riding the crest of a ninety-foot wave. The boat rides smoothly over the crest and begins a long descent down on the trailing edge of the wave, harmless because it doesn't break.

Ten hours later you reach the mainland. Half the beach has been washed away by the great wave.

The three of you jump out and pull the boat ashore. You get your film developed as soon as you get home. All your pictures came out—a shark, three of your friends from school, one of Mrs. Glass, two of Todd and Kyra, one of Arturo, one of Rosanna, three shots of a volcano— and eleven of dinosaurs.

The End

You don't think you can outrun a tyrannosaurus, even a young one. There are trees nearby, but if you tried to climb one you're sure the dinosaur would be able to pull you down before you could get out of reach.

You run for your life.

Todd and Kyra are throwing rocks at the tyrannosaurus, but it doesn't even seem to notice. It's almost upon you. What should you do?

If you dodge sharply to one side, turn to page 38.

If you reverse and try to dash between its legs, turn to page 102.

Perhaps it's the sulfurous smell in the air that wakes you, perhaps an insect bite. You're vaguely aware that you're lying in a meadow and that your arm is itching. You look around, trying to figure out where you are. The last thing you remember is eating that sandwich . . .

Drugged. No doubt about it. Lebeau's guards must have drugged you and left you out in this meadow last night.

You're jolted out of your thoughts by the sight of something moving on the plain in the early morning light. The neck and head of a sauropod are just visible over the foliage. A moment later you see more of them.

Lebeau asked you if you wanted to see the dinosaurs—now he's left you unprotected in their midst. You realize how ruthless, how insane, this man is—and how right Arturo was to warn you about him!

You shudder to think about what might have happened to your friends. Maybe there's still a chance you can find them. But you're sure that you must be trapped inside the electrified fence Arturo told you about.

Suddenly the ground shudders beneath you and tongues of fire leap from the summit of the volcano in the distance. Maybe it's about to blow. Or maybe it just behaves this way every once in a while. There's no way you can know.

Turn to page 7.

72

"But you'll be stranded!" you tell Arturo.

He shakes his head. "As long as the island doesn't blow, Rosanna can hire a helicopter to pick me up. Tell her I'll wait for her every day at the creek at noon."

"Good luck, then." You shake hands with him, then run back to where the others were waiting. But when you arrive you find that they've gone. They must have thought you'd decided to stay with Arturo.

You run down the path to the creek. It seems to go on and on, much farther than you'd expected. Finally, it ends at a little water hole. You realize you've gone the wrong way. You retrace your steps and take another path. But this too leads to a dead end. At last you reach a bluff from which you can look down at the sea. The Sabercraft is already half a mile offshore and moving away fast.

Turn to page 15.

"Let's go see Mr. Lebeau," you tell Kyra. "I think you're right. He's not going to hurt us."

You both start toward the headquarters building. Arturo reaches out to stop you. He grabs Kyra by the arm, but you manage to evade him. There's no way you can free your friend, so you run toward the building.

The headquarters has high concrete walls with flowering vines growing up the sides. A second-floor veranda provides a sheltered outdoor space with a view of the sea.

When you reach the door two guards armed with submachine guns come out to meet you.

"Where did you come from?" asks one, speaking with a French accent.

"I went down in the plane crash. My friends and I made it here in a life raft."

He motions for you to precede him through a passageway. You pass a checkpoint where another guard frisks you. He speaks for a moment in French on his walkie-talkie, then tells you to sit down and wait for instructions.

After about twenty minutes you're shown into an office. A slight, elderly man with wispy white hair looks up from the desk.

"I'm Claude Lebeau," he says. "Please sit down."

You sit in the chair facing his desk. On the wall behind Lebeau is a photomontage of the island, showing scenes of the volcano, the forests, and the tree-dotted plains.

Turn to page 106.

74

Kyra finally decides to try swinging over the fence. Todd will go first, then Kyra, then you.

Todd shinnies up quickly and starts rocking the tree. A coconut comes down, and you catch it. He keeps swaying the tree until he's swinging right over the top of the fence. He lets go, landing on the soft ground on the other side.

It's Kyra's turn. She shinnies up the tree and starts rocking it. The treetop sways back and forth. You and Todd yell encouragement from the ground, but Kyra's not heavy or strong enough to bend the treetop enough so she can jump. After a while she gives up and shinnies back down.

"There's no way I can make it," she says. "You go on, though. No use in us all being stuck here."

"I can't just leave you here inside the fence," you say.

"Look," she says. "If you and Todd can get to the mainland, maybe you can send a helicopter or something to save me. Otherwise the dinosaurs will get us both—if the volcano doesn't get us first."

You glance up at the volcano. Tongues of flame are leaping from the summit.

Turn to page 64.

Rosanna glances at Arturo, who is halfway to the top of the nearest ridge. "I can't just leave him here."

"You have no choice," you say. "He has no right to condemn you to death, or us either."

"I can't be absolutely certain that the volcano will blow," she says. "I just think it will."

"That's good enough for me," Kyra says. "Let's go!"

Arturo calls back from the top of the ridge. "This is incredible—a whole herd of triceratops! I'm going to film them. Come on up here everybody. This is the sight of your life!"

Turn to page 43.

"We've got to give Arturo one more chance to come with us," you say. You hurry off after Arturo. In a minute or so you reach the ridge where he is aiming his camcorder at a dozen or more triceratops, creatures about the size of large elephants. They have tanklike bodies and massive, four-foot-long horns. The herd includes two calves. One of them, no larger than a cow, is wobbling along as if it's just learning to walk.

You're about to speak to Arturo when another monster lumbers onto the plain. It's a tyrannosaurus sixty feet high, perhaps the fiercest predator ever to walk the Earth!

The tyrannosaurus edges toward the smaller of the triceratops calves, which has been lagging behind the others. If the adult triceratops formed a wall, their spiked horns would slash the underside of any tyrannosaurus that dared to attack. But they seem unaware of the enemy.

The baby triceratops doesn't see the tyrannosaurus either. With two or three great bounds, the monster reaches the calf and seizes it in its gigantic jaws. It holds its prey in place with its claws and rips it open with one swipe of its murderous teeth.

The calf lets out a scream as it dies. This noise is followed by a thunderous bellow from an adult triceratops. You watch in awe as this giant animal, perhaps the victim's mother, paces the ground and starts toward the tyrannosaurus, slowly at first, then with increasing speed.

Turn to page 104.

78

You're too stunned to talk as you gaze at the horrible sight around you. An oil slick and some scattered debris are the only signs that your plane ever existed. There doesn't appear to be a single other survivor.

When you've pulled yourselves together, you and your friends poke around to see what supplies are in the raft. You find drinking water and emergency rations, paddles, a six-foot mast, and a small, triangular sail. You start unfurling the sail.

"Wait," Todd says. "We don't want to sail anywhere. Search planes will be looking for us. We ought to stay as close to where we crashed as possible."

"I don't think so," Kyra says. "Our plane had changed course, and the radio was out—the search planes won't know where to look. Besides, the sunspots have knocked out navigation systems. We can't be that far from land. If we sail west, we'll get there. It's better than just sitting here!"

"You're supposed to stay with the wreck," Todd argues. "It's a basic rule of survival."

Kyra turns to you. "It looks like you have the deciding vote. What do you think we should do?"

If you vote for staying near the crash site, turn to page 109.

If you vote for sailing to the mainland, turn to page 8.

"If you're looking for the dinosaurs, don't worry," Arturo says. "There's an electrified fence separating the dinosaur reserve from the rest of the island."

"I'd like to see the dinosaurs," Kyra says, "but more than that, I want to get home."

"That won't be easy," Arturo says. "Claude Lebeau, who runs the institute, is planning to make a movie about the dinosaurs. He expects it to make a billion dollars in worldwide sales if no film or videotape gets out ahead of time. That's why he's doing everything in secret and has armed boats patrolling the island. And that's why if he catches you, he'll kill you. It would be an easy crime to conceal. Everyone would assume you were lost in the plane crash."

"He'd really do that?"

Arturo nods. "He's the most ruthless man I've ever met."

"But what about the volcano?" Kyra says. "We heard it might blow at any time."

"It might," Arturo says. "In fact, that's what Lebeau is counting on. All the dinosaurs will be killed and there will be no record left of them except the film footage that he and his crew take with them when the volcano erupts. He'll have a monopoly on the film and make a fortune."

"Lebeau sounds crazy," you say. "How many dinosaurs are there on this island anyway?"

Turn to page 22.

80

You take a deep breath. "I'm staying," you say. "I want to see these dinosaurs."

Kyra looks uncertain. "Well, if you two are staying, I guess I will too," she says finally.

The sun has almost set. You make camp for the night. Rosanna spreads out a drop cloth on the ground and Arturo rigs a rough tent out of mosquito netting. It's not very comfortable, but you're so tired that you sleep soundly. The next morning, Arturo has you all up early.

"We have a lot of ground to cover," he says. "Here's the plan." He points to Todd and Kyra. "You two will come with me to follow the electric fence to the left." He points to you. "You and Rosanna will follow it to the right. Remember, our goal is to get as complete a census of the dinosaurs as we can."

"But if the volcano acts up anymore, we should all break off research and return to this point immediately," Rosanna says.

"Okay, let's go!" Arturo straps on his backpack and leads Todd and Kyra eastward along the fence. You and Rosanna start off to the west.

Go on to the next page.

For the first quarter mile the area beyond the fence is obscured with thick tropical forest. Finally you reach an open vista. The two of you peer through the fence, Rosanna scanning the scene with her binoculars.

"If there are any dinosaurs in there, you won't need binoculars to see them," you say.

"Not so," she replies. "Some dinosaurs are only as big as chickens."

Turn to page 114.

Kyra looks doubtful. "Are you sure?"

"Positive," you say. "Do you want to go first, or should I?"

"You go," she says.

You wade into the water, crouch down, and do a shallow dive. The water is only a couple of feet deep under the fence. You keep your belly as flat and low as you can and make it through safely. Kyra follows close behind.

Once on the other side, the two of you follow the stream all the way to the sea. Then you walk

out to a little point so you can see up and down the coast as far as possible.

A fast-looking cabin cruiser is coming by. You duck down, thinking it might be Lebeau's, but then you notice that it's flying the Australian flag. You and Kyra jump up and wave frantically.

Go on to the next page.

84

There are two men in the boat. They see you and swing their craft toward you, bringing it up on the side of the point that's sheltered from the surf.

The sign painted on the hull says,

UNIVERSITY OF MELBOURNE
DEPARTMENT OF GEOLOGY

A lanky man is at the helm. "Get ready to come aboard," he says. "Is that all of you?"

"I'm afraid so," you say, "except for a friend of ours who was trying to get another boat."

Turn to page 65.

All kinds of thoughts race through your head, but the main one is that you've got to get off the island as fast as you can. But how?

If you run toward Lebeau's headquarters building, you might be able to reach his helicopter before it takes off. Maybe Lebeau would take mercy on you and give you a ride.

Or you could run down to the shore and try to find Arturo and the others. Then you could all escape together in the boat. Either way, you have to make a decision—now!

If you run toward Lebeau's headquarters, turn to page 62.

If you head for the beach, turn to page 90.

You know that the sharks could puncture the raft in an instant. Your only protection is that *they* don't know it. But that may not be enough. Another shark hits the raft, harder this time. You smack it on the head with a paddle, and it veers off.

"I don't know if that was a good idea," Kyra says. She points to the shark's fin, carving an arc through the water. "It's circling back."

"I'll just hit it harder," you say.

Todd grabs the other paddle. You brace yourself for the next attack. Fortunately it doesn't come. The sharks all swim away, perhaps sensing better game elsewhere.

The next morning dawns warm and hazy, with a strange, sulfurous smell in the air. The wind is blowing from the west. You see a smudge on the horizon in that direction.

"What's that smell?" Todd wonders aloud.

"It must be that volcano on Kirin Island," you say.

"I hope it doesn't blow," Kyra says.

"Look! More sharks!" Todd points to ripples in the water a few yards away.

Turn to page 98.

"There's one dinosaur that could get off the island," you say to Rosanna.

"It's not really a dinosaur," she says, "but a separate order. Anyway, look at the awkward way it flies. I doubt if it could make it more than a few miles over the ocean."

"Look!" You've spotted a pack of small allosauruses stalking a lone stegosaurus.

Rosanna nods. "Like wolves going after a moose," she says, pulling out her video camera. "A wolf looks for a chance to dart in and get at the moose's flank without getting its face kicked in."

She holds up the camera and starts filming. As she pans her camera over the scene, she rattles off descriptions into the recorder.

At that moment the earth trembles. You're almost knocked off your feet. Rosanna is thrown to the ground, camera still in hand.

The tremor passes.

White plumes of steam are rising along the base of the volcano. Rosanna gets to her feet and brushes off the dust.

"The gate we came through is closed. We don't have time to find another exit." She takes a large rubbery thing with a steel cylinder attached to it from her backpack. You realize that it's a balloon and a supply of compressed helium.

Turn to page 113.

When the cabin cruiser reaches shore, the two guards lead you to Lebeau's headquarters and show you into a large office in the rear.

"Here's the kid, Mr. Lebeau," one of them says.

A man in his sixties looks up from behind a large teak desk. He has keen blue eyes and wispy white hair. Sitting in a corner of the office, motionless but alert, are two Dobermans—either the ones that were guarding the dock or some just like them.

Lebeau motions for you to take a seat across from him. "How did you get on this island, and how did you get hold of my boat?" he asks in a thick French accent.

You explain about the plane crash. At first you don't mention Arturo, but when you realize that Lebeau will never believe you were able to take out the guard and the two dogs on your own, you tell him that a man helped you.

"Who?"

"I didn't get his name."

Lebeau stands up, his eyes flashing. "You're going to give us the truth. Do you want it to be painless, or . . . otherwise?"

The Dobermans are on their feet. Their eyes are fixed on you as they emit low throaty growls.

You decide to tell Lebeau exactly what happened.

Turn to page 48.

You race down to the creek. Kyra and Todd are already there.

"We thought we'd have to leave without you," Todd calls.

You don't have the breath to answer him, so you simply nod and help shove the boat into the water. You know it may be only minutes before the volcano blows.

The three of you jump into the boat. Kyra starts the engine and steers toward the mouth of the creek.

"Where's Arturo?" you ask.

Todd shudders. "It was horrible," he says. "He was scouting close to the fence while we watched him from the woods."

"One of Lebeau's guards shot him—just like that," Kyra finishes.

At that moment the boat reaches the turbulent waters where the creek meets the sea. You brace yourselves. For the next fifty yards your craft pitches wildly, plowing into rollers that break over the bow.

Kyra steers a steady course. In a few minutes you reach quieter water. She revs the engine and heads out to sea at top speed.

About twenty minutes later the sky lights up over the island. Heat, borne on a hurricane wind, sweeps over you. If it weren't for the flying spray you'd all be baked on the spot.

Turn to page 42.

You wave and shout, trying to get the men's attention. One of them sees you and taps the helmsman's shoulder, pointing at you. The boat slows and swerves toward shore.

Two of the men have their weapons trained on you. They hop out of the boat. One of them yells, "Drop your packs and come forward."

You do as he says.

"Where did you kids come from?" he asks.

"Our plane crashed," you reply.

"Are there other survivors?"

"We're the only ones as far as we know," Kyra says.

The men scan the beach, as if suspicious that she may be lying. "Seen anyone else on this island?" one asks sharply.

"No. We've only been here a few minutes," Todd says.

"Get your packs and help us turn this boat around. We're taking you back to the institute."

As the boat races back along the coast, its hull slaps against the waves, keeping you off balance. But you're glad to be going fast. You're impatient to get to where you can call your family and let them know you're alive.

Turn to page 12.

The sauropod is so colossal that it makes the trees, bushes, rocks, and birds around it seem as if they were in miniature. The huge dinosaur reaches her baby and swings her thirty-foot neck around it protectively, nudging it back from the fence. You're so fascinated that you take several more pictures of the scene.

"This is fantastic," Arturo says. "We never knew how nurturing dinosaurs were. I think they were much more like mammals than like ordinary reptiles."

You watch the dinosaurs until they pass out of sight. By that time darkness has overtaken you,

and Arturo and Rosanna decide it's time to make camp for the night.

You're exhausted and fall asleep quickly. When you awake in the morning, Arturo is already up and about. His eyes are trained on the volcano. Sparks mingle with the smoke pouring out of the summit. There's an acrid, sulfurous smell in the air.

Go on to the next page.

94

Rosanna crawls out of the makeshift tent and stands motionless, staring at the volcano. Then she reaches into her backpack and pulls out a small black box covered with knobs, buttons, and dials. She extends a telescoping metal rod from it and thrusts it into the ground. The needle on the dial starts quivering.

"She's measuring seismic waves," Arturo informs you. "It may mean something—only an expert can tell."

Rosanna studies the tiny movements of the needle.

Turn to page 60.

"Maybe there's fog because we're near shore," you say. "Have you heard any breakers?"

"Nope," Todd says. "And since there's nothing to do, I guess I'll try to get some sleep."

"Me too," you say. You curl up beside the others in the bottom of the raft and drift back to sleep.

The next sensation you have is one of rising in the air. You sit up and see that the raft is on the crest of a breaker. You're only a few dozen yards off a beach! There's a great roar of water, and the three of you are tossed into the sea.

You go under and come up just as another breaker is bearing down. You dive through it, surface again, and swim hard for the beach.

When you reach it, you spot Kyra nearby, struggling in the wash. You give her a hand, and the two of you make it up onto dry sand. Todd is already ashore.

"Where's our life raft?" he yells.

You see it for a second in the trough of the sea, drifting down the coast. It's lost, and all your supplies with it, unless it washes ashore.

Turn to page 16.

Lebeau shows you into a wood-paneled study lined with computers, video monitors, and other equipment. You stare for a moment at the realistic-looking model of a dinosaur on his desk.

"Sit down." He motions to the chairs opposite him.

You notice a pair of phones on the desk. "Sir," you say, "we'd like very much to call our families and let them know we're safe. Could we—"

"I'm afraid it's impossible," Lebeau interrupts. "Communications to the mainland are out because of very strong sunspot activity. I'll let you know when you can get through."

"Please, can't we try anyway?" Kyra says. "It's very important to us."

"We'll try as soon as it's possible," Lebeau says, smiling. But you find yourself wondering if he means it.

"When can we get back to shore?" you ask.

He picks up a phone and speaks to someone in French. "The helicopter is making a trip to the mainland early tomorrow. In the meantime, would you like to see some dinosaurs?"

You exchange glances with the others. "There really *are* dinosaurs here?"

"You'll soon see for yourself," Lebeau says.

"Why have you kept their existence such a secret, then?" you ask.

Turn to page 52.

"But the boat is risky too," Todd says. "If we're caught, we could die just as fast as if a dinosaur got us."

"I don't care. I want to try," Kyra says.

The idea of taking a boat and making a getaway appeals to you. You want to reach the mainland so you can call your family and tell them you're okay.

On the other hand, you'd love to get a look at those dinosaurs.

*If you decide to stay on the island,
turn to page 80.*

*If you decide to try to escape,
turn to page 27.*

You grab a paddle and watch the area. After a second something surfaces—but it's not a shark! The creature has a long neck and a small head with razorlike teeth. It stops and looks right at you, remaining just out of reach of your paddle. You get a glimpse of its thirty-foot-long body and four powerful flippers. Except for its elongated neck and reptilian head, it looks like a giant sea lion.

The creature submerges as quickly as it came.

"Was I seeing things?" Kyra says. "What was that?"

"This is what happens to people adrift at sea," Todd says. "They begin to—"

He cuts himself off. A brilliant flash of light has lit up the western horizon.

"It's the volcano!" you yell.

The flame slowly dims, and a plume of dense, yellow-black smoke spreads out over the region. The water between you and the smudge on the horizon takes on a white, frothy look. Suddenly you realize what's happening.

"The blast—it's coming toward us!"

You pull the storm cover over the raft and zip it shut, then huddle down with the others. Thirty seconds later the blast hits, accelerating the raft down a wave, rolling it over and over.

Turn to page 105.

100

The door slams in your face. You hear the lock turn. From somewhere out on the plain, you hear the bellowing of a dinosaur.

You run to the window. It's nailed shut. You look out into the darkness. All you can see is the dim silhouette of the trees outside.

You sit on the bed, dejected and confused. Was Arturo lying, or was Lebeau? Maybe they both were. At last, fatigue gets the better of you, and you fall asleep.

When you wake up, it's broad daylight outside. Over the treetops you can see the plume of smoke curling up from the summit of the volcano. The smoke looks denser than it did yesterday.

You hear a low rumbling sound. Is it the volcano or the dinosaurs? As you stare out the window you notice the wire mesh of the electrified fence through the gaps in the trees.

You try the door, but it's still locked. You knock, and a guard arrives and shows you to the bathroom. When you come out, he locks you in the room again but returns soon afterwards with a tray containing a couple of mangos, a stale bagel, and a cup of coffee. Once again you hear the lock click in the door.

Turn to page 5.

"I agree," you say. "We've got to find a place in the fence where we can get through."

"How?" Todd asks. "If dinosaurs can't get through it, I don't see how we can."

"We're smarter than dinosaurs," Kyra says.

You nod. "First we have to find the fence."

Everyone looks around. "Okay, let's fan out," Todd suggests. "I'll see what I can see from the top of that hill. Kyra, how about checking out the other side of that grove of trees?"

"I'll see what's beyond that outcropping," you say, pointing. "But we don't want to get too separated. Let's all be back at this spot in ten minutes."

The others agree. You start off, but a rustling among the trees startles you. You stop and listen. Could it be a small dinosaur? You decide it's probably just a bird.

A shrill cry rings out from the trees, quickly answered by another. Through the branches, you catch sight of a monkey swinging from limb to limb. It leaps and then is hidden from view. You relax. If other creatures can survive on the island of the dinosaurs maybe you can too.

Turn to page 116.

You boldly turn around and run straight at the young tyrannosaurus, diving between its legs. You're up in a flash, running in a crouch, dodging the gigantic tail.

Confused, the animal wheels and paws the air.

You glance around. Todd and Kyra are running toward a group of huge boulders. You race after them. The tyrannosaurus turns and starts after you.

Your friends have slipped into a crack between two large rocks. You dive in headfirst behind them, seconds before the tyrannosaurus arrives. The animal squats down and extends a tiny forearm into the niche.

The dinosaur's arm is only a couple of feet long, but it's tipped with vicious-looking claws. You, Todd, and Kyra squeeze together as tightly as you can, trying to avoid the daggerlike claw raking the air in front of your faces.

Your heart is already beating fast, adrenaline pumping through your body, when a thunderous roar fills the air. It's not the sound of a baby dinosaur, but of something far more awesome.

The claw withdraws from the niche. Edging forward, you can see the young tyrannosaurus moving away. You wiggle out of the niche and then duck quickly back in again. A few dozen yards away is a sixty-foot giant that could hold you, Todd, and Kyra in its jaws and swallow you all at once.

Turn to page 118.

104

With the calf still in its jaws, the tyrannosaurus wheels and begins its retreat. At the moment it's in no mood to fight. It just wants to find a good place to enjoy its meal.

But the triceratops charges at full speed, slashing one of its horns into the tyrannosaurus's great hind leg. The monster lets out a deafening wail, drops the calf, and turns on its attacker, felling it with a powerful snap of its deadly teeth.

Another triceratops charges. The tyrannosaurus wheels with astonishing speed, stopping the new attacker with a lethal kick. Two other triceratops are coming toward the great predator. But when they see the first two writhing on the ground, they stop short and back off.

The tyrannosaurus, its gored leg bleeding, seizes the carcass of the calf and limps away. Its dinner is assured, but if its wound becomes infected it may die.

The scene has hypnotized you so much that you've forgotten that you'd come to persuade Arturo to escape from the island. You grab his arm.

"Arturo, you've got to come with us. It's suicide to stay here."

He looks around, his face taut. "I don't want to be responsible for risking your lives. Go on with the others. I'm going to stay here and finish my work."

Turn to page 72.

At last the motion eases, leaving the raft right side up. Except for a few bumps and bruises, none of you is hurt.

You unzip the cover and look out. The sea is choppier than it was before, and smoke continues to spread out from the site of the volcano. There's no sign of the sea monster.

Three more days pass before you're finally rescued by a passing ship. When you ask the captain about the explosion, he tells you that the volcano destroyed the entire island. All that remains is a reef formed by the crater's rim.

Not surprisingly, he scoffs at your report of the sea monster. But later, when you get home, you find that its description exactly fits that of the plesiosaur, a thirty-foot-long reptile that lived over a hundred million years ago.

The End

"Well," Lebeau says, speaking in a thick French accent. "So you are a survivor of the crash. You were very lucky. Tell me who else from your plane was lucky enough to reach this island?"

"As far as I know, just my two friends from school," you say.

"Where are they?"

"Down on the beach." For a moment you wonder whether to tell Lebeau about Arturo and Rosanna. You decide to tell him everything except that Arturo was willing to help you steal the boat.

When you finish, Lebeau says, "Now you understand why I have such tight security here." He gives orders in French to a guard, who hurries off. "I've ordered my men to find these people and arrest them."

"But they're scientists," you say.

"Scientists? They are thieves and profiteers." He glares at you, his eyes bulging. "I'm engaged in a legitimate enterprise, and these people come to spy on me. I spend a hundred million dollars acquiring this island and setting up my facility, tens of millions more on research, and they want to take my profit away. They want to take pictures and sell them and make the money that should rightfully be mine."

Go on to the next page.

"But they say you're not going to let anyone see these dinosaurs. They say you're just going to keep taking pictures until the volcano blows, and then you'll let all the dinosaurs die."

Turn to page 30.

"I think you're right, Todd," you say. "We should stay as close to the wreck as possible."

The wind is blowing the raft slowly away from the crash site, so the three of you have to take turns paddling to stay near it. When you're not paddling, you lie back in the raft and watch the sky, hoping to see a plane.

No help comes before sunset, however, and you resign yourselves to a lonely night on the water, trying to sleep. In the darkness you lose all sense of where the plane went down and give up trying to stay at the site. There's nothing to do but wait for morning. You finally doze off into a fitful sleep.

You wake up with the newly risen sun in your eyes. Your two friends are still asleep. A stiff breeze is blowing, raising whitecaps on the sea. You sit up. A wave breaks against the raft. Heavy spray flies in your face and soon wakes up the others.

There's enough food and fresh water on the raft to last a week, but you decide to ration these supplies carefully. That's just as well, because there's not a plane or a ship to be seen all day long. Then, just before sunset, a new danger arises. A group of sharks appears and swims up near the raft. One of them nudges against it. Others circle, as if waiting for a moment to attack.

Turn to page 86.

You head the speedboat toward Venus, confident that you're aimed at the mainland. There's very little wind, the seas are calm, and the boat moves smoothly across the water.

Venus is slipping closer to the horizon. It's going to set very soon, so you pick a bright star above it to use as your new guide.

You're tired but so keyed up that you have no trouble staying awake and keeping the boat on course through the night.

Turn to page 119.

You and Kyra watch through the fence as Todd runs off.

"We can't just stay and wait for him," you say. "We've got to try to find our own way out."

"Let's go that way," she says, pointing east. "Away from the institute."

For the next hour or so you and Kyra follow the fence, sometimes walking alongside it, sometimes making long circuits around the heavy brush that lines it. All the while, you keep an eye out for more dinosaurs. Once you glimpse a herd of triceratops grazing. It's hard not to stop and watch them, but the smoke and flames coming from the volcano remind you that you'd better keep moving.

A half hour later you reach a stream that flows right under the electric fence.

"We're practically out of here," you tell Kyra. You hurry toward the fence and stand at the edge of the stream. The fence barely brushes the top of the water. "Just as I thought. We can swim under it."

"We might get electrocuted!" Kyra exclaims.

"I don't think so," you say. "The fence can't be electrified where water is flowing through it, or it would short out. The bottom section must be insulated."

Turn to page 82.

Rosanna applies the cylinder to the balloon, which rapidly inflates to a sphere about six feet across. Working swiftly, she unloads the cassette from her video camera and seals it in a thick plastic envelope. She ties the envelope to the balloon and immediately launches it into the air. The balloon rises rapidly, drifting off to the west toward Australia.

"Now, even if we can't escape, there's a chance the world may learn that there were dinosaurs on this island," Rosanna says. Then she sits down on a rock, arms tightly crossed, looking out over the plain.

"Aren't you going to take any more pictures?" you ask.

She shakes her head. "I might as well tell you —the volcano is at the critical point. It won't be long now."

"You're just going to sit here and wait for the end?"

"Right," she says, without even looking at you.

"Well, I'm not going to." You run down the slope, back toward the gate. It's open, and the guardhouse is deserted. Inside, the computer and the two-way radio are still on. You turn up the radio receiver and hear the voices of Lebeau's men. They sound panicked.

"Time's running out—we've only got five minutes at most."

"Get that pilot out here!"

Then the circuit goes dead.

Turn to page 85.

You've gone about two miles farther along the fence when Rosanna stops short and puts a finger to her lips. You look through the brush ahead and see a small metal building set only a few yards from the fence.

"That's probably a control station," Rosanna whispers. "There may be a guard inside."

The two of you sneak up to the building and peer in one of the small windows facing away from the reserve. A guard is hunched over a console.

"I wonder what he's doing," you say.

Rosanna trains her binoculars on him. "Playing a computer game," she says. "I guess real live dinosaurs aren't enough to hold his interest."

You circle around the back of the building. Turning the corner, you notice a gate in the fence. It's shut but not padlocked. "Look!" you whisper, pointing.

Rosanna's eyes light up. "Great!" she exclaims. "We can get inside the reserve. The guard's view of us will be blocked by the brush. Once we're inside let's hike up to the top of that hill. We'll be able to see a lot more up there than walking along the fence."

Turn to page 18.

Nothing happens for a few seconds. Then you see a ring of white water radiating out from the island.

"That's the blast—hurricane force!" Rosanna cries. "You can see when it's going to reach us. *Brace!*"

The wind blasts the boat, wrenching it, whipping it among the wave tops, driving green water aboard like breaking surf. You hang on for your lives.

The wind passes as quickly as it came, leaving the boat half submerged and bobbing crazily in the waves. Except for a few scratches and bruises, no one is hurt.

Turn to page 53.

116

Continuing on, you see a curious mound about four feet high. You climb up it and find that its center has been hollowed out and lined with twigs and branches. Inside are three eggs, each about the size of a football.

You look around anxiously, surprised that the nest is unguarded, wondering what giant creature may be nearby. Maybe this kind of dinosaur doesn't guard its eggs. But if not, wouldn't they be vulnerable to predators? Maybe something happened to the mother.

Todd, running down from the hill, interrupts your thoughts. "I found the fence," he calls. "I think we might be able to get over it."

You run toward him. "How?" you ask, panting.

"You'll see," he says. "I've got a plan. First, we've got to find Kyra. She should be back by now."

Then you see her, running toward you. Only fifty feet behind her is a young tyrannosaurus, about twenty feet high. Instinctively you pick up a rock, hurl it, and hit the monster right in the snout.

Seemingly more perplexed than angry, it stops and stares straight at you. You can sense its dull brain working, forming the connection between what happened and you.

Suddenly it charges.

Turn to page 69.

118

You, Todd, and Kyra all watch as the mother tyrannosaurus herds her baby away, nudging him roughly as he walks as if to scold him for doing something wrong. Maybe he shouldn't have been sticking his arm into a niche in the rocks. A snake might have been lurking there instead of three frightened kids.

"Todd, what's your idea for getting over the fence?" you ask after the huge creatures have disappeared.

"Follow me." He leads you and Kyra over the hill and down a slope. You can see the fence up ahead. It's about twenty feet high and made of steel wire mesh. A grove of coconut palms stands beside it.

"See that palm on the right?" Todd says. "My plan is to shinny up it. By the time I reach the top I'll be about ten feet higher than the top of the fence. Then I'll rock the tree back and forth, and when I'm over the fence, I'll jump down on the other side."

Todd's plan might just work, you think. But Kyra looks doubtful.

"I think I can make it up the tree," she says. "But suppose I don't rock it enough, or don't jump at just the right time? I could come down right on the fence."

"I know it's risky," Todd says. "But what other choice do we have?"

Turn to page 74.

Dawn comes, and with it, the low outline of land ahead. You're prepared to run the boat up on the beach, but about half a mile offshore you spot a fishing boat. You turn toward it and almost immediately run out of gas. The fishermen see you, however, and a short while later they pull alongside. They bring you aboard and take you to the nearest harbor. Once you're ashore, it takes about ten minutes to get your parents on the phone.

"This is wonderful," your father says. "It's hard to believe this is really you."

"There's something that's even harder to believe," you say. "I saw a dinosaur yesterday."

The words are hardly out of your mouth when you hear a distant explosion, so powerful you can feel it in your bones. A sudden wind off the water strikes you. Sea gulls scream. A tall plume of smoke is rising over the horizon. The volcano has blown, and the island of the dinosaurs and everything on it have been swept into the sea.

The End

ABOUT THE AUTHOR

EDWARD PACKARD is a graduate of Princeton University and Columbia Law School. He developed the unique storytelling approach used in the Choose Your Own Adventure series while thinking up stories for his children Caroline, Andrea, and Wells.

ABOUT THE ILLUSTRATOR

RON WING is a cartoonist and illustrator who has contributed to many publications. He has illustrated many books in Bantam's Choose Your Own Adventure series, including *You Are a Millionaire, Skateboard Champion, Vampire Invaders, Outlaw Gulch, Viking Raiders, You Are Microscopic, Surf Monkeys, The Forgotten Planet,* and *Secret of the Dolphins;* as well as titles in the Skylark Choose Your Own Adventure series, including *Haunted Halloween Party, A Day with the Dinosaurs, Spooky Thanksgiving,* and *You Are Invisible.* Mr. Wing now lives and works in Benton, Pennsylvania.